Designed by Gina DiMassi. Text set in Hoffmann Roman.
Library of Congress Cataloging-in-Publication Data   Rathmann, Peggy.   The day the babies crawled away / Peggy Rathmann.
p. cm.   Summary: A boy follows five babies who crawl away from a picnic and saves the day by bringing them back.
[1. Babies—Fiction. 2. Rescue—Fiction. 3. Picnicking—Fiction. 4. Stories in rhyme.] I. Title.   PZ8.3.R222 Day 2003   [E]—dc21   2002152002
ISBN 0-399-23196-X   10 9 8 7 6 5 4 3 2 1   First Impression

THE DAY
THE BABIES
CRAWLED
AWAY

PEGGY RATHMANN

ICE CREAM

PONY

G. P. PUTNAM'S SONS

NEW YORK

To my nieces and nephews,
who are my heroes,

A.J.	Emma
Robin	J.J.
Andy	Teagan
George	Seryn
Margaret	Charlotte
Crosby	and Sophie
Kaeli	

With special thanks
to the Kadifa kids
for lending a hand,

And to J.P., the one who got away

Remember the day
The babies crawled away?
We moms and dads were eating pies,
The babies saw some butterflies—
And what do you know?
Surprise! Surprise!
The babies crawled away!

Remember the way
You tried to save the day?
You hollered, "HEY!
You babies, STAY!"
But none of them did.
And some of them hid.
I SAY!
What a day
When the babies crawled away!

They crawled in the trees chasing bees.

They crawled in a bog chasing frogs.

They crawled in a cave—
You cried, "Babies, BEHAVE!"
But the babies loved bats,
So the babies just waved!

When the babies crawled out on a ledge,
You yelled, "Babies!
Don't crawl near the edge!"
But none of them heard—
At least, not the three
Who thought they were birds
And got stuck in a tree!

You yelled,
"I'll be there in a jiff!"
As you scrambled down the cliff—
AND YOU SAVED THE WHOLE CREW!
(Including the two
Who practically flew
Before landing on you!)
NICE PLAY!
What a day
When the babies crawled away!

But then—
My, oh my!
How those babies began to cry!
They were hungry, and tired,
And their little mouths were dry!

So you mashed them some blackberries
With droplets of dew,
And they took a short nap
In a big pile on you—
I SAY!
What a day
When the babies crawled away!

Remember the sling
You invented to bring them all back?
You borrowed their diapers
And tied them into a sack!
With lines made of vines,
It took quite a while,
But you and the babies
All rode up in style—
Hey, HEY!
What a day
When the babies crawled away!

Remember the way

They followed you home that day?

Through the cave and the trees,

On their brave, little knees,

Waving "bye-bye"

To the bats and the bees—

OKAY!

What a day

When the babies crawled away!

Remember how we cheered:
"HIP! HIP! HURRAY!
You've fetched
Our darling babies
Home to stay!
You are our hero—
Have some pies!
And we insist
You've won FIRST PRIZE
For saving the day
When the babies crawled away!"

Remember the way
I carried you home to bed?
You were thirsty, and tired,
And your little eyes were red.
You told me your story,
I brewed you some tea,
Then you fell
Fast asleep
In a small pile on me . . .

Shhhhh!
I say,
What a day
When the babies crawled away.